For All
Para Todos

Alejandra Domenzain

Katherine Loh
Illustrator

"As an immigrant myself, the book brought tears of joy thinking of the thousands of young 'Flors' who will see themselves in this book and realize they too can make a difference."

– Julieta Garibay, Co-founder of United We Dream

"...a beautiful, powerful book... This is a great tool for educators and will inspire children to share their stories...should be in every library, school, and home."

–Julie Su, US Deputy Secretary of Labor

"...bilingual, full of hope and important lessons... It's a book that goes out from one heart to another. Yes, it's a children's book, but it moves us all."

–Jorge Ramos, Writer/Anchor Univision News

"Alejandra gives us a gift of courage and endurance... A magnificent book and model for all ages, schools and communities."

–Juan Felipe Herrera, Poet Laureate of the USA

"This bilingual book with a focus on immigrant rights is very relevant and urgent for our times...It will empower them to go beyond physical borders to become effective collaborators, global thinkers, border crossers, and creative geniuses."

–Dr. Santiago Wood, Executive Director,
National Association of Bilingual Educators

"This timely book captures the hidden realities faced by immigrants, and lifts up their brave efforts to pursue justice for all. A must read for our times."

–Teresa Romero, President, United Farm Workers

...a tender and captivating story about a migrant family and their journey for justice...a needed addition to the many literary voices we must raise to stop the criminalization of migration."

–Aida Salazar, award winning author of *Land of The Cranes*

"*Para Todos* is a gift to the world...it will make you smile, cry, and reflect, and it will teach the little ones how migration is a difficult act rooted in love and dreams."

–María Gabriela "Gaby" Pacheco, Program Director,
TheDREAM.US; first undocumented Latina to testify before Congress

"Lyrically written for kids of all backgrounds, *For All* is a riveting story that is more important than ever in these times.

–Innosanto Nagara, author of *A is for Activist*

"Joyful, inspiring, uplifting and real. *For All* is a hero's journey for our times. A needed story for every American family who believes the enduring symbol of our country is not the barbed wire fence; it is the Statue of Liberty."

–Martin O'Malley, 61st Governor of Maryland

"*For all/ Para Todos* is an intimate view of the dreams, aspirations of Dreamers and also their struggles and heartbreaks. Everyone should read this book before they opine on the fate of Dreamers."

–Carlos Gutierrez, former U.S. Secretary of Commerce

"The book thoughtfully reflects the reality of millions of people across the United States whose story rarely gets told."

–Duncan Tonatiuh, award winning author of *Undocumented: A Worker's Fight; Separate is Never Equal*

"Stories like this allows us to have a real conversation about the humanity, courage and resilience in the immigrant community. That's exactly what we need in this moment to be able to change the hearts and minds of the American public on this issue."

–Erika Andiola, Chief Advocacy Officer, RAICES

"...a beautifully written book for children and adults alike and will be instrumental in helping new generations understand what immigrant children and their families experience."

–Marielena Hincapié, Executive Director, National Immigration Law Center

"The story...effectively emphasizes some basic, persistent fears of struggling immigrant families...simple, sparsely colored illustrations... add richness to the tale."

–Kirkus

"*For All/Para Todos* is a revolutionary story about a young girl's pursuit for justice. This book is perfect for readers of all ages because it offers lessons that are valuable in any stage of life.

–LitPick

"This beautifully written bilingual book gives voice to the experience of so many people... For students and for their parents and teachers, *For All/Para Todos* is a rich resource for conversation, validation, and inspiration."

–Dr. Deborah Palmer, Professor, Equity, Bilingualism and Biliteracy, University of Colorado, Boulder

"If we are ever to live up to our ideals as a nation of immigrants, it'll be due to more teachers and parents teaching, and children learning, the timeless lessons in *For All/Para Todos*."

–Charles Kamasaki, Senior Advisor at UnidosUS, Fellow at the Migration Policy Institute, author of *Immigration Reform: The Corpse That Will Not Die*

"An important contribution–very few children's books address health and safety issues faced by workers today, and also how immigrants are fighting for their rights!"

–Jessica Martinez, Co-Executive Director of the National Council for Occupational Safety and Health

For All/Para Todos, Copyright © 2021 by Alejandra Domenzain

Illustrations Copyright © 2021 by Katherine Loh

ISBN: 978-1-7344938-7-0

Illustrations by Katherine Loh

Translated by Irene Prieto de Coogan

Book Cover and Interior Design by Denise Shavers

Published by Hard Ball Press. Information available at: www.hardballpress.com, info@hardballpre
Hard Ball Press, 415 Argyle Rd., 6A, Brooklyn, NY, 11218

Library of Congress Cataloging-in-Publication Data:

Domenzain, Alejandra, For All/Para Todos. 1.Children's Literature, 2. Immigrant Rights,
3. Immigration, 4. Crossing Borders, 5. Coming of age

For my father: Thank you for giving me deep roots in Mexico and
a chance to blossom in the United States.

For my mom: Thank you for giving me the courage to use my green pen.

For Gabi: Thank you for being my companion in activism and in life.

Para mi papi: Gracias por darme raíces profundas en México
y la oportunidad de florecer en los Estados Unidos.

Para mi mami: Gracias por darme la valentía de usar mi pluma verde.

Para Gabi: Gracias por ser mi compañera en el activismo y en la vida.

Irene Prieto de Coogan and Alejandra Domenzain
Translators

This is the story of a girl named Flor –
Why she came to this land, and what happened before.
Her country was right next to this one, and yet
It seemed just as far as you could possibly get.
Flor learned from TV about life on "that side,"
Staring in wonder with eyes open wide.
People there, it appeared, owned oh so much stuff!
While for her there was usually never enough.

Esta es la historia de una niña llamada Flor –
De dónde vino y cómo llegó acá: Dos países vecinos
¡Tan distantes!
Por la tele Flor aprendió sobre la vida en "el otro lado"
Con ojos muy abiertos veía que allá la gente
Parecía tenerlo todo, mientras que en su casa
Rara vez había lo suficiente.

1

When she saw TV shows that had Christmas with snow,
Kids opening gifts in the tree's cozy glow,
She dreamt of bright gifts piled high on the floor,
When you thought you were done, there was always one more!

As she put on her clothes and combed her black hair,
She'd chat with her dad about life "over there."
"Do you know they have so many dresses and shoes,
That they're late every day cuz it's so hard to choose!"

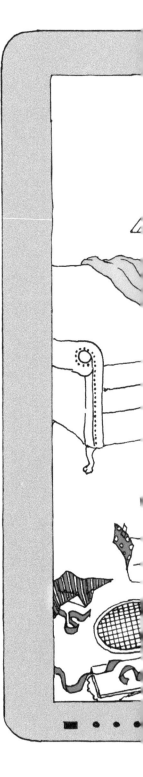

Al ver en la tele una Navidad con nieve
Y niños que abrían paquetes a la luz del arbolito
Flor soñaba con pilas de regalos brillantes
¡que nunca terminaba de abrir!

Mientras se vestía y peinaba su pelo negro,
Hablaba con su papá de cómo era la vida "allá".
"Tienen tantos vestidos y zapatos, Pa,
¡Que llegan tarde porque no pueden decidir cuál ponerse!"

Flor dreamt of that place where if you had sorrow,
You always believed in the hope of tomorrow,
Where the endings were happy and teeth gleamed so white,
No one was hungry and the law made things right.
One day her dad said, "Flor, we're leaving our land.
The fields have all turned into dust and dry sand.
We cannot grow corn with so little water.
Our land cannot feed us, my dear darling daughter."

Flor soñaba con ese lugar
Donde las penas se convertían en esperanza
Con finales felices y dientes blanquísimos
Donde nadie pasaba hambre y las leyes eran justas.
Un día su papá le dijo: "Flor, mi niña,
Tenemos que irnos de aquí.
El campo está seco; el maíz no crece.
Nuestra tierra ya no puede darnos de comer".

"Can't you find other work? Get a job in the factory?"
"I've tried," said her dad, "It was unsatisfactory.
The machines and the chemicals fill me with fear,
At work mom got sick after only a year!
I couldn't save her, but can save you my dear.
You're all that I have, and I can't raise you here."

"Are we going to the land that we see on TV?
Will we fly in a plane? Will there be toys for me?"
Her dad forced a smile and put on a brave face,
"It won't be so easy to get to that place.
It's a risk, I've been told, but we just have to take it;
They say over there, those who work hard can make it."

"¿No puedes trabajar en otra cosa? ¿Ir a una fábrica?"
"Ya traté. Hay máquinas y productos químicos que me llenan de
temor.
¡Tu mamá se enfermó al trabajar ahí solo un año!
No pude salvarla, pero te salvaré a ti, m'ija.
Eres todo lo que tengo y aquí no te puedo criar".

"¿Vamos a ese lugar que vemos en la tele?
¿Iremos en avión? ¿Tendré muchos juguetes?"
Su papa sonrió a medias y se armó de valor.
"No será fácil llegar. Me han dicho que hay riesgos,
Pero los enfrentaremos. Dicen que allá
Los que trabajan duro pueden salir adelante".

"They call it For All, *Para Todos*, because there,
All hard workers are given a chance, fair and square.
The people that built it came from all different places
It's clear when you look at their skin and their faces.
The world's yummiest foods are found everywhere,
And all the world's languages float in the air."

"If we're homesick," said Flor, "we can always come back."
"I'm not sure about that." Father's voice seemed to crack.
They walked around knowing this would be their last time,
First to the tree where Flor learned how to climb,
Then to the spot where her mother was buried.
"Who'll pull out the weeds and bring flowers?" she worried.

"Lo llaman *Para Todos*, porque a todos
Los buenos trabajadores se les trata con justicia.
La gente que construyó ese país llegó de todas partes;
Ya verás la variedad de colores de piel y de caras
Y de sabrosas comidas de todos lados que se pueden probar.
Allá se hablan todos los idiomas del mundo".

"Si extrañamos nuestra tierra, siempre podremos volver", dijo
Flor.
"No sé…" la voz del padre pareció quebrarse.
Dieron un último paseo hasta el árbol
En el que Flor aprendió a trepar. Y el sitio
Donde estaba enterrada su madre.
"¿Quién arrancará la maleza y le traerá flores?"
Preguntó con voz triste.

8

She looked at her home with a last, loving glance;
Dad said, "We must go while we still have the chance.
No matter what happens, wherever we live,
Be proud of our family, we have so much to give."

The journey was tiring, dangerous and long,
But Flor and her father had hope and stayed strong.
There were deserts and rivers and caves and a train.
They drank water from puddles and washed in the rain.

Vió con aprecio a su hogar, una última vez.
Papá dijo: "Tenemos que irnos mientras podemos.
Pase lo que pase, vivamos donde vivamos
Siéntete orgullosa de tu familia,
Pues es mucho lo que tenemos que ofrecer".

El viaje fue cansado, peligroso y largo,
Pero a Flor y su padre
La esperanza les dio fuerza.
Pasaron por desiertos y ríos, cuevas y un tren.
Bebieron agua de charcos y se lavaron con la lluvia.

They made it, feet blistered, their clothes more like rags,
And stared up in awe when they saw the great flags.
The stripes of *For All* waved high in the air,
They seemed to announce, "We all come from somewhere,
But now that you're here, we're one land united."
As they got to the gate, Flor was proud and excited.

Llegaron con los pies adoloridos y la ropa desgarrada.
Contemplaron las grandes banderas, asombrados.
Las franjas de *Para Todos* ondeaban muy alto en el aire.
Parecían anunciar: "Todos venimos de alguna parte
Pero ahora que han llegado formamos una tierra unida"
Al llegar al portal, Flor sintió orgullo y emoción.

The guard at the gate asked, "Where were you born?"
When dad answered, he gave him a look of great scorn.
He gave Dad two papers; Dad squinted his eyes.
Did Dad understand them? Were they a surprise?

Flor asked, "Why'd we get those? What do they say?"
"Don't worry," Dad said, and he put them away.
Flor had glimpsed a red X, but did not tell her dad.
Had they done something wrong? In school X's were bad.

El guardia de la entrada preguntó: "¿Dónde nacieron?"
Cuando Papá respondió, lo miró con desdén.
Le entregó dos papeles; Papá parpadeó.
¿Entendía lo que decían? ¿Se sorprendió?

Flor preguntó: "¿Qué son esos papeles? ¿Qué dicen?
¿Porqué nos los dieron?"
"No te preocupes", dijo Papá y los guardó.
Flor llegó a ver una X roja, pero no dijo nada.
¿Habían hecho algo mal? En la escuela eso quería decir la X roja.

11

When they finally arrived at their new destination,
It was not what Flor dreamt in her imagination.
Their apartment was small, with no garden, no pool,
She felt lost and alone in her strange, big, new school.

Dad came home every night
so achy and weary,
Played songs from his past, which made him get teary.
"Are you hurt? Are you sad?
Dad, are you okay?"
"Let's rest now, my love,
it's been a long day."

Cuando al fin llegaron a su destino,
Nada fue igual a lo que Flor imaginó.
El departamento era pequeño,
sin jardín ni alberca,
Y se sintió perdida en su nueva escuela,
Grande y extraña.

Papá llegaba a casa de noche, adolorido y cansado,
Tocaba canciones de su pasado que lo hacían llorar.
"¿Qué te duele, Papá? ¿Estás triste, te sientes bien?"
"Vamos a descansar, mi niña, ha sido un día muy largo".

Flor found it hard to learn a new language.
Her lunch felt all wrong; couldn't Dad make a sandwich?
Flor tried to blend in, being lonely felt sour,
She said to her class, "My name's Flor, which means flower."
Kids exploded in laughter, "You're named after the floor!"
Flor's cheeks turned bright red and they giggled some more.

Flor knew other kids came from far away too –
Was it easier for them? Did they know what to do?
Every day Flor could feel her heart and head ache.
Was coming to For All one big bad mistake?

Se le hacía difícil a Flor aprender el idioma nuevo.
Su almuerzo era diferente a los demás; ¿por qué no podía
su papá hacerle un sándwich?
Sintiéndose sola, trataba de adaptarse.
Dijo en la clase: "Me llamo Flor".
Los niños rieron: "¡Te llamas como el piso!"
Flor se puso roja y ellos se rieron más.

Flor sabía que otros niños también venían de lejos.
¿Les era más fácil? ¿Sabían qué hacer?
A Flor le dolía el corazón y la cabeza,
¿Había sido un gran error venir a *Para Todos*?

One day during recess, Flor sat on the grass.
Ms. Soto came out from her language arts class.
She saw Flor was adrift and said "You're not alone,
Your story reminds me a lot of my own."
Flor said, "It's so hard, they don't understand."
"I do," said Ms. Soto, taking Flor's hand.
"I started like you, coming here was a struggle.
You'll soon feel at home."
She gave Flor a snuggle.
"When I was your age and was stuck,
I would write,
And words would reach
into the dark like a light.
I want you to have this green pen,
for I'm sure
That writing will help you stay
strong and endure."

Un día Flor estaba en el patio a la hora del recreo
Cuando Ms. Soto salió de
su clase de lenguaje,
Vio que la niña se sentía perdida
y le dijo:
"No estás sola.
Tu historia me recuerda la mía".
Flor dijo: "Es tan duro, no me entienden".
"Yo sí", dijo Ms. Soto,
tomándole la mano.
"Empecé como tú, con muchas dificultades.
Pero pronto te sentirás en casa", dijo abrazándola.
"Cuando tenía tu edad y me sentía así,
Me ponía a escribir,
Y las palabras iluminaban la oscuridad.
Quiero darte esta pluma verde, porque estoy segura
De que escribir te ayudará a ser fuerte y aguantar".

Flor began writing, first choppy and slow,
But soon words gushed forth, filling row after row.
She wrote of her journey, the things left behind.
She wrote of her dreams, all she hoped she would find.
She could finally explain with the help of her pen
How you ache and you grow when you're starting again.

Ms. Soto said, "You have a story to tell.
I'm sure other students have felt this as well.
Put it in the school paper for others to read.
Your words will help others who are also in need."
And it did! Kids came up and told Flor, "We read it,
We feel the same way, and we're so glad you said it."

Flor empezó a escribir, primero lenta y trabajosamente.
Pero pronto las palabras surgieron, llenando los renglones.
Escribió sobre el viaje y lo que dejó atrás,
Sobre sus sueños y sus esperanzas.
Al fin podía explicar, a través de su pluma,
El dolor y el crecer que vienen al comenzar de nuevo.

Ms. Soto le dijo: "Tienes una historia que contar.
Estoy segura de que otros estudiantes han pasado por lo mismo.
Ponla en el diario escolar para que la lean.
Tus palabras les servirán.
¡Así fue! Otros niños se acercaron a Flor: "Leímos lo que escribiste,
hemos sentido lo mismo.
¡Gracias!"

Flor ran straight back home to tell Dad all about it.
Things will get better! She wanted to shout it.
But Dad wasn't home, again working late.
Flor stared at the window, it was so hard to wait.
As night fell, she realized, "I don't know where Dad is,
I wrote down my story, but I don't know his."

When dad came home tired and sat down to unwind,
Flor asked all the questions she had on her mind.
"Why are you so tired, with no time for fun?"
Dad said, "Work is hard when you're out in the sun."

"Last Christmas, you said we couldn't go shopping.
Why don't you have money if you work without stopping?
Your jobs are so hard, it doesn't seem fair,
The boss takes the money, why can't he share?"

Flor corrió a casa a contárselo a Papá.
¡Todo va a ser mejor! Quería decirle.
Pero Papá no había llegado aún; de nuevo trabajaba tarde.
Flor miró por la ventana, la espera se le hacía larga.
Se hizo de noche. "No sé dónde está Papá.
Escribí mi historia, pero no conozco la suya".

Papá llegó cansado y se sentó.
Flor le hizo todas las preguntas que quería:
"¿Por qué estás tan cansado, sin tiempo para divertirte?"
"Es duro trabajar bajo el rayo del sol", dijo él.

"En Navidad dijiste que no podíamos ir de compras.
¿Por qué no tienes dinero, si trabajas tanto?
Tu empleo es muy duro, no es justo.
El jefe gana todo, ¿por qué no lo comparte?"

19

Dad looked at Flor, his eyes crinkled with pain,
He said, "There is something I have to explain.
Remember those papers we got long ago?
I tried to protect you, but it's time that you know."

He took out the papers they'd gotten before.
With a low, trembling voice, he read one to Flor.
"To all those that come to *For All*, be advised,
Here are the rules so you won't be surprised:

Papá miró a Flor con pena.
"Tengo que explicarte algo.
¿Recuerdas los papeles que nos dieron hace tiempo?
Yo quería protegerte, pero es hora de que lo sepas".

Sacó los papeles y con voz temblorosa
Leyó para Flor:
"Los que llegan a *Para Todos*, sepan
Que estas son las reglas:

You can pick the strawberries or pounds of tomatoes,
Clean up the bathrooms and fry the potatoes,
You can't get more money or work without pain,
You'll get into trouble if you dare to complain.
If you do, guards will come, in no time at all.
We can have you locked up and removed with one call."

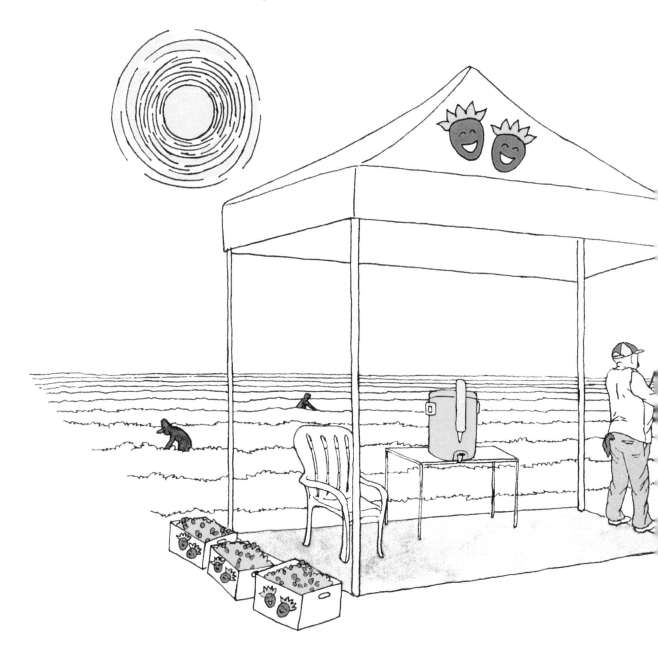

Podrán recoger fresas o libras de tomates,
Limpiar baños y hasta freír papas.
Pero no podrán ganar más ni trabajar sin dolor.
Les irá mal si se atreven a quejarse.
Llegarán de inmediato los guardias
Y con solo una llamada podemos meterlos
a la cárcel o deportarlos".

"So if you speak up, they can take you away?"
"Yes Flor, I have to just do what they say.
I know it's not fair, but I do it for you:
If you study, then there's so much more you can do!"
Her dad seemed to trust things for her would be better,
But Flor was afraid there was more to this letter.
She saw one more page which her dad didn't mention.
Was that page about her? Flor swallowed the question.

"Entonces, si te quejas, ¿te pueden llevar?"
"Así es Flor, tengo que hacer lo que me piden,
Sé que no es justo, pero lo hago por ti:
Si tú estudias, ¡podrás lograr mucho más!"
Papá parecía creer que las cosas serían mejor para ella,
Pero Flor temía que la carta dijera algo más.
Vio una página que Papá no mencionó.
No se atrevió a preguntar: ¿tenía que ver con ella?

Flor put her green pen away, far out of sight.
It wasn't enough to tell stories and write.
Dad couldn't speak up, it wasn't allowed.
It was safer for her to blend in with the crowd.
Flor needed to use all her determination
To get into school for a good education.
For her next school, a test would decide,
If Flor knew all the answers, they'd let her inside.
Every day Flor would study, learning slowly but steady,
And when the test came, she was totally ready.

Flor escondió su pluma verde. Entendió
Que no bastaba con escribir historias.
Papá no podía quejarse.
Era mejor que ella se adaptara:
Necesitaba poner todo su empeño
En adquirir una buena educación.
Un examen decidiría si Flor podía pasar a la siguiente escuela.
Si sabía todas las respuestas, entraría.
Flor estudiaba a diario, aprendiendo poco a poco, sin parar.
El día del examen, estaba lista.

She'd done it, her dad had been right to believe!
For All really gave her the chance to achieve.
The school would accept her with one big hurray,
Flor planned her first day and what she would say:
"I'll go to this school to invent a new pill
To help mothers like mine if they ever get ill.
And to have a fair job, not like those of my dad,
Then I'll buy him the things that he's never had."

¡Lo había logrado, Papá tenia razón!
Para Todos le había dado esta oportunidad.
La escuela la aceptaría con aplausos.
Flor pensó en lo que diría al llegar:
"Entraré a esta escuela para inventar una medicina
Que ayude a madres como la mía si se enferman
Y para conseguir un trabajo justo, no como los de Papá.
Así podré comprarle a Papá todo lo que nunca ha tenido".

When she got to the school, she saw a big sign:
If your papers have check marks, go stand in that line.
If they have a red X, that means you should go,
We cannot accept you, the answer is no.
The guard said, "I know your test score was great,
But the orders I have say DON'T OPEN THE GATE.
If you were born here, then you belong,
If you were not, you'll always be wrong.
Our grandparents weren't born here, yes that is true,
But we must draw the line, and we draw it at...you!"

Al llegar a la escuela vio un gran letrero:
"Si sus papeles tienen una señal de aprobado
Fórmense en esa fila.
Si tienen una X roja, no los podemos aceptar
Y tendrán que irse".
El guardia dijo, "Aunque estudiaste mucho y tus notas son excelentes,
Tengo órdenes de NO ABRIRTE LA PUERTA.
Si naciste aquí, perteneces.
Si no, nunca te aceptaremos.
Cierto que nuestros abuelos no nacieron aquí.
Pero hay que poner límites y el límite para ti es....este".

Flor ran to her father and asked, "Did you know?
Did that paper list places where I cannot go?"
"Yes, Flor, it said, 'To all those that come
Know 'justice for all' means 'justice for some.'
For me it means jobs with hard work and low pay.
For you, I guess schools will now send you away.
I hoped that, with time, we would both be accepted,
You'd be let in, and I'd be respected.'"

Flor corrió a buscar a su padre:
"¿Sabías que en ese papel se habla de lugares
A los que yo no puedo entrar?"
"Sí, Flor. El papel decía: Todos los que llegan aquí sepan
Que 'justicia para todos' significa 'justicia para algunos'.
Para mí, trabajos duros y mal pagados.
Para ti, ser rechazada de la escuela.
Yo tenía la ilusión de que con el tiempo seríamos aceptados:
Tú podrías pertenecer, yo sería respetado".

Flor said, "Oh Dad, I have so much to learn,
You believed in *Para Todos*, and now it's my turn.
I have to help those in the same situation;
Immigrants long to belong to this nation.
I think that the problem is people don't know
That workers are tired, youth have nowhere to go.
If they heard all our stories, I think they'd agree
To be fair to the immigrants like you and like me!"

Dad said, "I am scared, speaking out can be tough,
But you're right, working hard just isn't enough.
We need to convince them to make a new rule,
To work without fear and be let into school."

Flor dijo: "Ay, Papá, tengo mucho que aprender,
Tú creíste en *Para Todos*, ahora me toca a mí.
Tengo que ayudar a otros en la misma situación:
Los inmigrantes quieren pertenecer a este país.
El problema es que la gente no sabe
Que los trabajadores se agotan y los jóvenes
No tienen a dónde ir.
Si supieran todas nuestras historias
Creo que estarían de acuerdo
En ser justos con inmigrantes como nosotros".

Papá dijo: "Tengo miedo, no es fácil hacerse oir.
Pero tienes razón, no basta con trabajar duro.
Tenemos que convencerlos para que haya nuevas leyes,
para trabajar sin miedo y poder ir a la escuela!"

Flor remembered Ms. Soto and all her advice,
She grabbed her green pen without thinking twice,
She'd write down the stories of people she'd met
Who hadn't been able to speak up just yet.

She started with Dad's and wrote it all down,
Then she interviewed immigrants all over town.
"I'll go on TV to get out the word,
Tell voters the truths that haven't been heard!"

Flor se acordó de Ms. Soto y su consejo,
Volvió a tomar su pluma verde:
Escribiría las historias de la gente que había conocido,
Que todavía no habían podido expresarse.

Empezó por su padre y lo escribió todo.
Enseguida fue a entrevistar a los inmigrantes del pueblo
"¡Hablaré en la tele y diré a los votantes
Las verdades que no han escuchado!"

The man at the station asked, "Why are you here?
People like you never dare to come near."

"There are so many stories that I have to offer
About the unfairness that immigrants suffer.
Your viewers need to know the truth when they vote.
They might change their minds when they hear what I wrote.
If they know what it's like, I trust that they'll care,
Vote for schools for all kids and jobs that are fair."

"¿Qué haces aquí? La gente como tú
No se atreve a acercarse".

"Son tantas las historias que puedo contar
Sobre las injusticias que sufren los inmigrantes.
El público debe saber la verdad antes de votar….
Tal vez lo que he escrito les haga cambiar de opinión.
Si se enteran de lo que ocurre, estoy segura
De que decidirán votar por escuelas para todos
Y por trabajos justos".

Long ago, Flor had seen *For All* on TV,
Now she knew that *For All* wasn't all it should be.
But this was her home now, she felt loyal and proud,
So she had to speak up, say her truth right out loud.

Flor went on TV and got people's attention.
She got them to listen and also to question.
"Immigrants should not be abused and left out,
Justice must be what this country's about."

Tiempo atrás, Flor había visto *Para Todos* en la tele,
Ahora entendía que en *Para Todos* no era todo como debía ser.
Pero ahora este era su hogar y se sentía leal y orgullosa,
Y por eso tenía que decir la verdad.

Flor se presentó en la tele delante de todos
Y consiguió la atención del público;
La escucharon y se cuestionaron.
"Los inmigrantes no debían sufrir abusos ni exclusión,
Este país debe definirse por ser justo".

When Flor finished talking, people called on the phone,
Saying, "We feel the same! You aren't alone.
We also believe we can make this place better.
United, we'll change unfair laws all together."

Flor couldn't believe it, there were so many others
Who stood up for each other, like sisters and brothers.
They told her, "We know we are all one community,
We are strong only if we believe in our unity."
So Flor joined with the group to give a big speech,
And together their voices had a much wider reach.

Cuando Flor terminó de hablar, la gente empezó a llamar:
"¡Sentimos lo mismo! No estás sola.
Nosotros también creemos que unidos
Podremos cambiar las leyes injustas".

Flor apenas podía creerlo, había tantos otros
Que se apoyaban como hermanos y hermanas.
Le dijeron: "Sabemos que formamos una comunidad,
Y que nuestra fuerza será nuestra unidad".

"You inspired us all to vote for new rules
We'll win justice for all in our jobs and our schools!"

What do you think is right in this situation?
Should immigrants have a fair chance in this nation?
Should all kids have schools where they study for free?
And workers get paid so they live comfortably?

Le dijeron: "Nos has inspirado para votar por leyes justas
Para todos, en la escuela y en el trabajo".

¿Tú qué piensas de todo esto?
¿Crees que los inmigrantes deberían tener una oportunidad
en este país?
¿Debería haber educación gratis para todos
Y empleos bien pagados?

One day you will vote and make that big choice,
So be ready to answer and lift up your voice.
But for now, Flor's going around giving out pens,
Even Dad's started talking 'bout rights with his friends.

Your moment will come, though you may not know when –
So why not start writing, pick up your green pen!

Un día te tocará votar y tomar esa gran decisión,
Así que prepárate para hacerte oír.
Por ahora, Flor va repartiendo plumas,
Y hasta Papá se ha puesto a hablar de derechos con sus amigos.

Tarde o temprano llegará el momento para ti.
¡Toma tu pluma verde y ponte a escribir!

About the issues in this book

Historically, people from all over the world have come to the United States for many reasons. When European settlers came, they pushed out the indigenous people living here out of their homes and killed many others. Africans were kidnapped and brought here to work as slaves. People from many countries came to do crucial work that sustained the economy and built the culture of this country for hundreds of years. Many others have come fleeing war, poverty, and unfair treatment. In some cases, the United States has been directly or indirectly responsible for the conditions that caused people to flee their homes. For example, the U.S. government has funded and supported violent governments and set up trade agreements that contribute to poverty in other countries.

Immigrants still do many important and tough jobs, but often they don´t get paid enough to meet their basic needs and face conditions that put at risk their safety and health. They are often threatened that if they speak up, they will lose their job or be deported (sent to the country where they were born against their will), no matter how much they have contributed to this country. In spite of this, immigrant workers have fought for fair working conditions and have made big changes.

Some immigrant children grow up as members of this country, but face limitations for being undocumented (not having the right papers to give them permission to live here). There are many things undocumented people can't do, including voting, getting a driver's license, and getting a loan or scholarship to pay for college. They live in constant fear that their families will be separated, and that they will lose everything they have worked for. Many young people who were brought here as children have joined together and organized to demand fair treatment. This could include a chance to get the papers they need to study, work, vote, and live in the country they c home without fear of being deported.

In recent years, children coming to this country have been separated from their relatives by U.S. immigration officials and put in separate detenti facilities, making it hard for families to re-unite. Both children and adults are being locked up in unsafe conditions for long periods of time, often in ways that harm them and violate their rights. If Flor and her father had come to the U.S. in th past few years, they may have been separated from each other, and this would have been a different story.

Many people welcome immigrants who are their neighbors, teachers, friends, caretakers, grandparents, and life partners. Most people war to fix our unfair immigration system. This could mean making sure those who come here can do s safely and with permission, giving those without documents a chance to get them, and making sur that all people who live here have basic rights. It could also include making sure those who come are treated fairly and are in safe conditions until it is decided whether they can stay. Some people feel threatened by immigrants because they seem different or because they fear immigrants will commit crimes or take others´ jobs, even though evidence does not support this. In every generatio there has been fear about new immigrants. Often the children and grandchildren of immigrants worry about new immigrants coming in, even though most immigrants are an integral part of o culture, economy, and society.

Many decisions will be made regarding the rights of immigrants in this country. Undocumented people are not allowed to vote, so citizens have a big role to play in making these decisions. However, the courageous actions of people like th racters of Flor and her father have convinced many voters that immigrants deserve to be respected, appreciated, recognized, and given the same opportunities as those born here. Also, many believe that immigrants are what make this country uniquely rich in its culture, vibrant in its growth, and alive with people who dream and build. For more information about the book, see www.forall-paratodos.net

Discussion questions

Flor and her dad decide to go to For All because there are no jobs in their country. What are other reasons why immigrants leave their home?

What are Flor's expectations of life in For All? How does the reality differ from what she dreamed about?

The dad did indeed find jobs in For All, but they were probably not what he had hoped for. Why?

Ms. Soto plays an important role in the story. What does Flor learn from her?

What is the role of writing and story-telling in this book?

How does Flor try to convince people to vote for fairness for immigrants? What other arguments could she make?

Flor feels that loving her new home means telling hard truths to help make it a better place. Do you think it's patriotic to try to change things that seem unfair to you?

Flor notices that stories of undocumented immigrants are not told from their point of view on TV (or other media). Why does this matter?

9 The dad chose to remain quiet and obey the instructions on the papers (until he decided to speak up at the very end). Why do you think he made that choice?

10. The X on the papers in this story stand for a kind of "deal" that's made with immigrants— on the one hand they are needed to work and they make great contributions to For All. In this sense, they are members or "citizens." One the other hand, they do not have the right papers or permission to be here. How could this be solved?

11. Flor found a group of people who also wanted to make change. What is the advantage of taking action with others?

12. The green pen represents your voice to tell stories and advocate for justice. What do you want to do with your green pen?

Sobre los temas en este libro

Históricamente, personas de todas partes del mundo han venido a los Estados Unidos por muchas razones. Cuando vinieron los inmigrantes de Europa, sacaron de su hogar a las personas indígenas que vivían aquí y mataron a muchas más. Los Africanos fueron raptados y traídos aquí para trabajar como esclavos. Hay personas de muchos países que han venido a hacer trabajo esencial que sostuvo la economía de este país y creó su cultura por cientos de años. Muchos otros han venido huyendo guerra, pobreza y trato injusto. En algunos casos, los Estados Unidos ha sido directamente o indirectamente responsable por las condiciones que causaron que las personas huyeran de su hogar. Por ejemplo, el gobierno de los Estados Unidos ha dado dinero y apoyo a gobiernos violentos y ha establecido acuerdos de comercio internacional que contribuyen a la pobreza en otros países.

Los inmigrantes todavía hacen muchos trabajos importantes y difíciles, pero muy seguido no les pagan suficiente para cubrir sus necesidades básicas y enfrentan condiciones que ponen en riesgo su salud y seguridad. Muy seguido los amenazan que si se quejan, perderán su trabajo o los deportarán (los mandaran al país donde nacieron en contra de su voluntad), sin importar cuánto han contribuido a este país. Sin embargo, los trabajadores inmigrantes han luchado por condiciones de trabajo justas y han logrado cambios grandes.

Algunos niños inmigrantes se crían como miembros de este país, pero enfrentan limitaciones por ser "indocumentados" (no tener los papeles adecuados dándoles permiso de vivir aquí). Hay muchas cosas que las personas indocumentadas no pueden hacer, como votar, tener una licencia para conducir y obtener un préstamo o beca para pagar la universidad. Viven con el miedo constante de que sus familias pueden ser separadas y que pueden perder todo lo que habían logrado. Muchas personas jóvenes que vinieron aquí de niños se ha juntado y organizado para exigir un trato justo. Esto puede incluir la oportunidad de conseguir lo papeles que necesitan para estudiar, trabajar, vota y vivir en el país que consideran su hogar sin mie a ser deportados.

En los últimos años, los niños que han venido a este país han sido separados de sus parientes por autoridades de inmigración de los Estados Unido y los han puesto en centros de detención separad lo cual hace difícil que se puedan reunir. Están encarcelando a niños y adultos en condiciones inseguras por periodos de tiempo largos, muy seguido en formas que les hacen daño y que viola sus derechos. Si Flor y su papá hubieran venido a los Estados Unidos en los últimos años, esta hubiera sido una historia muy diferente.

Muchas personas les dan la bienvenida a los inmigrantes que son sus vecinos, maestros, amigo cuidadores, abuelos y compañeros de vida. La mayoría quiere arreglar nuestro sistema de inmigración injusto. Esto puede incluir asegurars de que los que vienen aquí pueden hacerlo de forma segura y con permiso, dar a los que no tie documentos la oportunidad de conseguirlos y asegurarse de que todas las personas que viven a tienen derechos básicos. También puede incluir asegurarse de que los que vienen son tratados de una forma justa y están en condiciones seguras hasta que se decide si se pueden quedar. Algunas personas se sienten amenazadas por los inmigran porque parecen ser diferentes o porque temen qu los inmigrantes van a cometer crímenes o quitar trabajos a los que viven aquí, aunque la evidencia no lo respalda. En cada generación, ha habido miedo de los inmigrantes nuevos. Muy seguido, l hijos y nietos de los inmigrantes están preocupad por los nuevos inmigrantes que llegan, aunque la mayoría de los inmigrantes forman una parte integral de nuestra cultura, economía y sociedad.

chas decisiones se harán sobre los derechos
los inmigrantes en este país. A las personas
ocumentadas no se les permite votar, entonces
ciudadanos tienen un papel muy importante en
nar estas decisiones. Sin embargo, las acciones
ientes de las personas como los personajes de
r y su papá han convencido a muchos votantes
los inmigrantes merecen ser respetados,
apreciados y reconocidos y que debemos darles
las mismas oportunidades que reciben los que
nacen aquí. También muchos piensan que los
inmigrantes son lo que hacen que este país sea
único por su riqueza cultural y crecimiento
constante, energizado por las personas que sueñan
y construyen. Para más información sobre el libro,
vea www.forall-paratodos.net

reguntas para discusión

Flor y su papá deciden ir a *Para Todos* porque
no hay trabajo en su país. ¿Cuáles son otras
razones por las cuales los inmigrantes dejan su
hogar?

¿Cuáles son las expectativas de Flor para la vida
en *Para Todos*? ¿De qué forma es diferente la
realidad de lo que ella había soñado?

El papá sí encontró trabajo en *Para Todos*, pero
no era lo que había esperado. ¿Por qúe?

La Señora Soto tiene un papel importante en la
historia. ¿Qué aprende Flor de ella?

¿Qué papel juega el escribir y contar historias en
este libro?

¿Cómo es que Flor trata de convencer a otras
personas a que voten por la justicia para los
inmigrantes? ¿Qué otros argumentos podría
hacer?

Flor siente que el amar su hogar nuevo quiere
decir que debe decir la verdad aunque sea difícil,
ayudando así a mejorar el país. ¿Tú crees que
es patriótico tratar de cambiar las cosas que te
parecen injustas?

8. Flor se da cuenta de que las historias de los
indocumentados no se cuentan desde su punto
de vista en la televisión (o en otros medios de
comunicación). ¿Cuál es la importancia de esto?

9. El papá decidió quedarse callado y obedecer las
instrucciones en el papel (hasta que decidió alzar
su voz al final). ¿Por qué crees que tomó esa
decisión?

10. La X en los papeles en esta historia representa
un tipo de "trato" que se hace con los
inmigrantes. Por un lado, los necesitan
para trabajar y ellos hacen contribuciones
importantes a *Para Todos*. En este sentido, son
miembros o "ciudadanos". Por el otro lado,
no tienen los papeles correctos o el permiso
de estar aquí. ¿Cómo se podría resolver este
problema?

11. Flor encontró un grupo de personas que
también querían lograr cambios. ¿Cuál es la
ventaja de actuar junto con otras personas?

12. La pluma verde representa tu voz para contar
historias y abogar por la justicia. ¿Qué quieres
hacer con tu pluma verde?

ALEJANDRA DOMENZAIN grew up in Mexico and the United States. She has been an advocate for immigrant workers for over 25 years, and also worked as an elementary school teacher. Currently, she is dedicated to improving workplace health and safety for low wage workers. Alejandra is using her green pen to write books that invite kids to question, dream, and stand up for justice.

ALEJANDRA DOMENZAIN Se crió en México y los Estados Unidos. Ha abogado por los trabajadores inmigrantes por más de 20 años y también fue maestra de primaria. Actualmente, se dedica a mejorar la salud y seguridad laboral para los trabajadores de bajos ingresos. Alejandra está usando su pluma verde para escribir libros que invitan a los niños a cuestionar, soñar y defender la justicia.

IRENE PRIETO DE COOGAN was born in Mexico City. She earned her BA in French Literature at UNAM (Universidad Nacional Autónoma de México), and later her MA in Latin American Literature at Hunter College. Irene came to New York to work as translator for the UN Conference Services, and is now retired. She writes prose and poetry, and so far has published: *Los Poemas de Irene* (1990), short stories in *Hecho(s) en Nueva York* (1994), and a second poetry collection *Mujer de Otro País* (2018).

IRENE PRIETO DE COOGAN nació en la Ciudad de México. Se graduó con una licenciatura en literatura francesa de la UNAM (Universidad Nacional Autónoma de México) y después con una maestría en literatura latino americana de Hunter College. Irene fue a Nueva York a trabajar como traductora para el Servicio de Conferencias de las Naciones Unidas y ahora está jubilada. Escribe prosa y poesía y hasta ahora ha publicado *Los Poemas de Irene* (1990), historias cortas en *Hecho(s) en Nueva York* (1994) y una segunda colección de poemas: *Mujer de Otro País* (2018).

KATHERINE LOH is an artist, illustrator, and muralist who believes that art can be a powerful tool for social dialogue and political change. She began her discovery of social justice through art while working with community arts organizations in San Francisco. Now, she is working to introduce art as a tool for social impact and community empowerment from Switzerland, where she is presently based. Website: katherinepaints.com

KATHERINE LOH es una artista, ilustradora y muralista que cree que el arte puede ser una herramienta poderosa para el diálogo social y cambio político. Empezó a descubrir cómo lograr la justicia social a través del arte mientras estaba trabajando con una organización comunitaria de arte en San Francisco. Ahora, está trabajando para introducir el arte como una herramienta para impacto social y empoderamiento en Suiza, donde está basada actualmente. Website: katherinepaints.com

HARD BALL & LITTLE HEROES PRESS
Stories to Change the World
Children's & Young Adult Books

The Cabbage That Came Back, Stephen Pearl (Author), Rafael Pearl (Illustrator), Sara Pearl (Translator)

Down on James Street, Nicole McCandless (Author), Byron Gramby (Illustrator)

For All/Para Todos, Alejandra Domenzain (Author), Katherine Loh (Illustrator), Irene Prieto de Coogan (Translator)

Freedom Soldiers, a YA novel, Katherine Williams (Author)

Good Guy Jake, Mark Torres (Author), Yana Muraskho (Illustrator), Madelin Arroyo (Translator)

Hats Off For Gabbie!, Marivir Montebon (Author), Yana Murashko (Illustrator), Laura Flores (Translator)

Jimmy's Carwash Adventure, Victor Narro (Author), Yana Murashko (Illustrator), Madelin Arroyo (Translator)

Joelito's Big Decision, Ann Berlak (Author), Daniel Camacho (Illustrator), Jose Antonio Galloso (Translator)

Manny & the Mango Tree, Ali Bustamante (Author), Monica Lunot-Kuker (Illustrator), Mauricio Niebla (Translator)

Margarito's Forest, Andy Carter (Author), Allison Havens (Illustrator), Omar Majeia (Translator)

Polar Bear Pete's Ice Is Melting! (A 2021 release) Timothy Sheard (Author), Kayla Fils-Aime (Illustrator), Madelin Arroyo (Translator)

Trailer Park, JC Dillard (Author), Anna Usacheva (Illustrator), Madelin Arroyo (Translator)